Neptune's Gift

Discovering Your
Inner Ocean

I hope you find your
inner ocean in these pages!

Peace,

Scarlet
3/14/19

Neptune's Gift
Discovering Your
Inner Ocean

iUniverse, Inc.
New York   Bloomington

Neptune's Gift
Discovering Your Inner Ocean

Copyright © 2008 by CJ Scarlet

iUniverse books may be ordered through booksellers or by contacting:

iUniverse
1663 Liberty Drive
Bloomington, IN 47403
www.iuniverse.com
1-800-Authors (1-800-288-4677)

ISBN: 978-0-595-52785-4 (pbk)
ISBN: 978-0-595-51550-9 (cloth)
ISBN: 978-0-595-62838-4 (ebk)

Printed in the United States of America

iUniverse rev. date: 11/20/08

*T*he middling wave bobbed contentedly on the ocean surface. The sun shined gloriously overhead, casting a dazzling carpet of twinkling diamonds across the surface of the blue-green water. A cool, westerly breeze chased wispy white clouds across the late autumn sky. Seagulls with black-tipped wings swooped and danced high in the air in daring aerial maneuvers. Pelicans with feathers the color of wet driftwood dived into the water with great splashes, scooping fish into their beaks and rising triumphantly with their catches. A pod of dolphins leaped in synchronistic joy, laughing and urging one another to play.

Dylan, an average dull gray wave living an average life, always waited with excitement for the ocean to exhale and send him rushing forward in the water. He especially loved to have the winds carry him high into the air, lifting him toward the sun and the open, endless blue of the sky. In these blissful moments, Dylan felt most happy and alive. Somehow, in a way he couldn't quite define, when soaring above the peaks he felt as if he were mysteriously connected to some magnificent force.

It bothered him very much that he couldn't stay at those wonderful peaks. At just two-and-a-half feet above the surface, Dylan longed to hold a commanding view of the ocean around him. Nevertheless, no matter how hard Dylan tried to stay on top, he always found himself back in a trough, unable to see the horizon, afraid he would be trapped there forever. On dreaded days, ominous black and blue clouds covered the sun and pelted the ocean with stinging rain, whipping him and the other waves into a confused jumble.

When the dark times ended, as they always did, Dylan felt immensely relieved and jubilant. He stretched his crest toward the welcoming rays of the sun and breathed deeply of the crisp, salty air, grateful to be back on top. Dylan kept himself so busy trying to reach the peaks and avoid the troughs that he never paid attention to the peace that abided quietly in the middle, the comfort zone of the present moment.

Dylan tried very hard to be satisfied with his up and down life, but he craved something more. He was surrounded by magnificent, breathtaking waves. Dylan watched with admiration and envy as the big waves rose, arching majestically into the sky. As they reached their peaks, they tossed glistening droplets high into the air that caught the light and created veils of rainbows that slowly settled back into the sea.

More than anything else in the world, Dylan wanted to be magnificent and breathtaking too. When he regarded his dull gray wave and pale gray foam, he felt washed out and insignificant. The middling wave could not imagine that he, in fact, glistened with his own magnificence.

One day, a strange wind ruffled the surface and Dylan felt a sense of dread. He peered out across the sea and saw ominous black clouds racing toward him. The wind picked up, and without warning, a monstrous hurricane swallowed the ocean in one massive gulp. The savage storm's harsh winds howled furiously, turning the sea into a raging torrent and terrifying the middling wave, whose tossed foam turned an ominous dark gray under the screaming sky. Dylan held on for dear life, tumbling and whirling up and over and around the other waves, crashing, choking on foam, struggling for air.

The hurricane was so powerful that it tore waves from the sea. So loud, it thundered in Dylan's crest, stealing the middling wave's fearful cries and flinging them into the uncaring wind. Dylan felt helpless, out of control, unable to find his bearings. He huddled together with a group of other waves and fought to hold his crest above the chaos, terrified that at any moment he would drown. Dylan cried out to King Neptune to save him and prayed for the hurricane to end. After a long, terrifying night, the hurricane's fury abated, leaving Dylan exhausted.

Ever since that petrifying night, Dylan lived in constant fear of another ferocious hurricane, and he began to notice a queasy, anxious feeling when he fell into the troughs. When he was trapped in those depressions, he felt as if he would never again see the sun, just like the pale, blind fish that lived in the darkest reaches of the ocean floor. Although the dolphins begged Dylan to play and the cormorants tried to cheer him up by splashing around in his crest, Dylan felt sad and hopeless. Nothing seemed to lift his spirits. He felt weighed down by the ghosts of storms past and by his desperate longing for the elusive, cherished peaks.

Dylan tried to rise higher by gathering momentum from the other waves around him, but they wanted to be big waves themselves and resisted his efforts. He and the other waves jostled about, pushing and pulling, competing with one another as they fought for power and energy.

Sometimes other waves shared their energy and helped lift Dylan a bit higher, making him feel loved and supported. Other times, just as he was on the rise, his fellow waves thwarted his attempts, leaving him feeling small and unappreciated.

But Dylan kept trying to be greater, no matter what the wind and the other waves threw at him.

Thoughts to Play With

Think of a time in your life when you felt stuck in a trough, unable to see the horizon.

How did you feel? Isolated and lonely? Sad and depressed?

Did it seem like your life would never be happy again?

Remember how time and courage led you back to a state of balance and contentment.

Now recall a moment in your life when you felt connected to a larger force in the universe.

Take a deep breath, close your eyes, and remember. How did you feel in that mystical moment when you felt connected, felt part of the *One*? Did you experience joy? A sense of wonder and peace?

Do you wish you could experience these precious moments of connection more often?

One breezy morning, as Dylan was watching a flock of red-billed terns soar in lazy circles in the sky above, he heard a loud scream just behind him.

"Aaaaaaahhhhhhhh!" the sound rose as another, slightly larger wave came crashing down right on his head! Dylan and the larger wave tumbled over and around each other in a mad rush. When Dylan collected himself, he looked angrily at the larger wave.

"You clumsy oaf! What are you doing?" Dylan yelled. Although he was generally a very polite wave, Dylan didn't much like surprises, and his voice was defensive and gruff.

"So sorry," the other wave mumbled in a quivering voice as he tried to back away in a vain attempt to flee. Dylan pushed back against him in confusion.

"Excuse me, but you're heading in the wrong direction," Dylan said crossly.

"No, I'm not! I'm trying to escape!" the other wave shouted frantically.

"Escape what?"

"Certain death!" the wave howled, his voice hoarse with terror.

Shocked, Dylan asked, "What in the ocean are you talking about?"

"I just had a glimpse above the other waves in front of us. They're crashing on the shore! We're all gonna die!" The larger wave wailed, flailing about in panic.

Dylan felt a deep sense of dread. He grabbed onto the larger wave, keeping it from moving past him.

"What do you mean we're all going to die?" he demanded loudly, trying unsuccessfully to keep the anxiety out of his voice. Dylan had heard rumors of a terrible shore that devoured waves. He always thought the scary tales were just stories told by big waves to keep the little waves in line.

"I mean we're going to be pulverized! Torn asunder! Ripped to shreds! Smashed to smithereens! We're going to DIE!" Shaking with terrified sobs, the other wave began to hyperventilate and gasped for air.

"That's...that's just a stupid myth," Dylan stammered fearfully, hopefully.

The larger wave grabbed Dylan and screamed in his face, sending foamy spittle into his eyes. "There *is* a shore and all the waves *are* crashing on it, and *we're* going to crash too unless we flee out to sea!"

The other wave tried again to push past Dylan, but the force of the other waves drove him back. He cried out in frustration and anguish. Dylan heard his cries fade into the wind as he lost sight of him.

Was it true? Was there really a terrible shore? Were all the waves really crashing into it? Was he really going to be wiped out? Dylan shuddered with fear.

No way, he thought. But Dylan's stomach sank with dread as he envisioned himself smashing against the voracious shore. The reality of the whole situation hit Dylan like a tsunami, crushing his spirit the way the shore would soon crush him. He suddenly felt very alone, as if he were the only wave in an uncaring ocean.

There wasn't a cloud in the sky. The sun still beamed and the gulls still circled and the dolphins still danced, but Dylan could appreciate none of them. The temporary happiness of the peaks was pointless now. The troughs he dreaded so much seemed even more daunting and deep.

Dylan tried to recall the joy and exhilaration he experienced when he soared at the top of the peaks, when he felt so much a part of one mysterious, joyful force. But now that he knew he was going to wash out soon, the world had lost its beauty. Dylan grew ill and listless. The cold water sliced through him and sea salt stung his wounds.

Desperately, Dylan wanted some wave, any wave, to comfort him, to make him feel better, to lead him back to the peaks. But the other waves either didn't notice that he was suffering, or they didn't care.

Dylan wondered why King Neptune had abandoned him. He wept bitter tears of loss and frustration.

Thoughts to Play With

Everyone encounters situations that seem overwhelming, and sometimes we let our dramas take over our lives and thwart our happiness.

Have you ever had your dreams of greatness shattered by reality? Have you felt separated, fragmented, disconnected from a larger, loving force or universe?

What challenges have you experienced that changed how you perceived your future? Can you see how those challenges led you to greater strength and wisdom?

Take a moment to appreciate your courage and resiliency, and know that life will never give you more than you can handle. You are part of a loving universe that wishes to serve you.

$\mathcal{D}$ylan bobbed and waved as he always had, but his heart just wasn't in it. He felt angry and resentful toward the waves behind him for the time they had that he did not. Even Dylan's desire to be a big, beautiful wave dimmed over time. It wasn't that he didn't *want* to be big and beautiful; it just seemed that he was only a middling wave, and he believed he had neither the time nor the ability to reach his cherished goal.

As the ocean rolled ponderously beneath him, Dylan tried even more desperately to cling to the peaks, and was even more disappointed when he dipped into the troughs. Staring dully at the sky, Dylan watched the cormorants and pelicans glide in freedom overhead. He envied their safety up in the air and wished he could fly too. Sometimes Dylan roiled with jealousy at the birds for reminding him of the watery chains that held him to the sea. He would never reach as high as he had once dreamed.

One day a quick, fierce storm churned up the waves. The storm was over in a flash as it swept away, Dylan ran smack into a big, beautiful wave, sending foam and sea spray in every direction.

"I'm so sorry," he said, bowing low to the big wave.

"That's all right. You didn't hurt me a bit," she said, smiling kindly.

"How could I?" Dylan asked, looking downcast. "I'm just an average wave. I could never have an impact on a magnificent wave like you."

The big wave looked at him with concern. "You seem very sad," she observed. "What's the matter?"

"I'm sad because I'm going to crash onto the shore," Dylan said morosely, weeping salty tears.

"I see," she said. "And why does that make you sad?"

Dylan blinked in disbelief. "Because I will cease to exist! I will leave the surface of the ocean and be gone forever!" He waved his froth dramatically about to make his point.

The vibrant blue wave laughed, confusing Dylan even further. "You silly droplet," she smiled gently. "You aren't merely a wave! Don't you know that?"

Dylan was caught off guard and suddenly unsure of himself. "I thought I was just an ordinary wave," he said in a tiny voice.

"Where in Neptune's ocean did you get such an idea?" she asked.

"Well, look at me," Dylan said. "I'm a wave. This is my middling crest and this is my plain old foam and these are my dull water droplets. I'm not big or beautiful, and I can't touch the sky or make rainbow veils like you do."

"And?"

"And, my crest is separate from your crest and that crest and that crest way over there," he explained impatiently, pointing to waves a bit farther out. Dylan lowered his crest and heaved a defeated sigh. "We're all separate from each other."

The beautiful big wave looked amazed. "You mean all this time you thought you were only this little wave right here, all alone on the surface of this tiny patch of ocean?"

"What else *is* there for me to be?" he asked.

The beautiful wave shook with warm laughter, flinging snowy white foam in all directions. Dylan looked up at her brilliant droplets and felt a stab of envy. The large wave was so much taller—almost ten feet tall!—and so magnificent it took his breath away. He felt embarrassed and even more insignificant rolling, so pitifully small, next to her.

Seeing his distress, she tried to put him at ease. "Let me introduce myself. I'm Serena." She beamed a friendly smile. "Who are you?"

"My name is Dylan," he answered shyly. "It means 'child of the ocean.'"

"Hello, Dylan," Serena smiled even wider. "I'm so pleased to meet you."

Dylan bowed again.

"Forgive me for laughing, Dylan," Serena said. "I wasn't making fun of you; I was just surprised by what you said. But if you really believe you're just a solitary little wave, I can see how you would think you're going to fade away when you meet the shore."

"How can I think any differently?" Dylan asked. "I *am* going to crash on the shore and that will be the end of me." He let out a resigned sigh.

"That's not true, Dylan. I mean it *is* true that you're going to wash to shore, but that won't be the end of you; it will be a reunion." Serena offered him a reassuring smile.

Dylan was mystified. "A reunion with what?"

"With your true nature!" Serena proclaimed.

"My true nature?" Dylan asked, puzzled. "I don't know what you mean."

"Your true nature is who you really are, beneath the surface," Serena explained.

"And who am I?"

"Why, Dylan, you're the ocean!"

Dylan looked at Serena, his big eyes full of wonder and hope. "Really. *I'm* the ocean?"

Serena smiled and nodded. "You most certainly are."

Dylan said slowly, "So, if I'm a wave and you're a wave, and if I'm the ocean, then you are…"

"I am the ocean too!" she smiled radiantly, making a graceful bow over the small wave.

He frowned. "I'm confused. How can we both be the ocean. We're two different waves. I don't see how we can be the same thing."

"Separation is an optical illusion, my friend. Your eyes see only the superficial differences between us, leading you to think we are unconnected," Serena said patiently, rolling slowly at his side.

Dylan shook his crest. "That may be true for you; you're a big, beautiful wave. You don't know how lonely and terrible the ocean is for the average wave."

"I am *exactly* like you, Dylan." Serena tilted her crest and looked at him with a calm, clear gaze. "After all, I'm part of the ocean too. I've crashed on the shore many times. Yes, I'm bigger, but otherwise we are the same."

Dylan looked at Serena with skepticism. She could see that he didn't believe he was the ocean and not a mere wave, separated from everyone else. Serena tried a new tack. "Look closely at your crest," she said.

Dylan did his best to look around, unsure of what he was looking for.

"Can you see the water droplets in your crest and inside your wave?" Serena continued, "Each one is its own little world, with a separate view of its tiny life. From their perspectives, these droplets appear to be separate from one another, but in fact, each one is part of you; they are what make you into *one being*."

Serena watched as Dylan closely examined his crest, his foam, and his bubbles. He couldn't see the individual droplets, although he knew they were there. He hadn't thought about it before, but Serena was right; all those separate droplets combined to make him one wave.

"It's the same for you and me," Serena explained. "You and I have separate views of the world and appear different, but we both are actually elements of the ocean — we are *one* with the ocean. A trillion bubbles, a million waves, one ocean."

Dylan frowned as he struggled to make the connection between the way the droplets formed him and the way the droplets of all the waves made up the ocean. "I can see how I am made up of individual droplets," Dylan said slowly, "but I'm having trouble seeing myself and the other waves in the same way. I don't feel connected to them at all." He felt a strange ache in his heart and wished he could feel like he truly was one with all of them.

Seeing his morose expression, Serena shared her compassion for Dylan once again. "Tell me, Dylan, can you show me where in the water you end and I begin?"

Dylan looked at the trough between them, searching for the place where his wave stopped and hers started, realizing it was impossible to find. He sighed and admitted, "No, I can't."

"That's right, because there *is* no end to you and no beginning of me. There is a constant, endless flow that moves within us and between us, and between every other wave on the ocean, too." Serena looked warmly at her new friend. "All of our waves mingle and influence one another."

"But I can't help but see you and the other waves as different from me," Dylan persisted, looking frustrated.

"As long as you cling to your belief that you are separate, you will be. Your mind will reject any evidence to the contrary. But if you look for the connections, you'll see them all around you." Seeing Dylan's quizzical look, Serena said, "Let me give you an example. Tell me, have you ever seen a waterspout?"

"Yes, a long time ago," he said, recalling the fascinating white tornado of water that hovered above the ocean surface until it evaporated.

"When a waterspout races across the ocean, it appears to be different from the water below it, because it has taken on a different form. However, the waterspout—just like your wave—is merely a swirling movement of ocean water that has been stirred up by the wind. When the wind dies down, the spout disappears back into its source." She waited patiently for Dylan to absorb her words.

At that moment, a gust of wind threw a veil of Serena's sea foam into their air, creating a quick rainbow that disappeared almost instantly. Dylan thought about how those rainbow droplets had been just ordinary droplets a moment before.

"I think I'm beginning to understand what you're saying, but I still feel so alone," he said pitifully. "The ocean is so big and I'm so small!"

"You are never alone, Dylan. *Never*," Serena assured him. "I can understand why it seems that way if you are focused solely on your own wave. Nevertheless, we are the same, not just as waves, but also as creatures of nature. The lobsters and starfish and plankton; the dolphins and sharks; the coral and cuttlefish—we are all *one*," she said, her crest shining brightly in the sun.

"Expand your awareness of others and you will begin to

feel your connection to all beings."

Thoughts to Play With

The universe and everything in it is made up of pure energy. We are *one* with the Source of all life.

Can you see your connection to other people and to every living thing in the world?

You have much in common with others. We all want to be happy and don't want to suffer, we all want to be recognized as unique, but we crave connection with others.

Like the waterspout and the ocean, living beings come in myriad forms, but we are all dependent upon one another for our survival.

Today, pay close attention to the people around you and try to acknowledge the things you have in common. This will help you to be more patient with others and appreciate them more.

Think of someone close to you, someone you feel connected to. Call them right now and tell them how much they mean to you.

"Why is it so hard to understand that I am connected to all beings?" Dylan asked with exasperation. "And if we're all one, why do I feel even more alone when I'm in the troughs?"

"You feel alone because your worry and sadness keep your attention on what's inside your mind, which is fear and hopelessness," Serena explained. "This anxious thinking cuts you off from everyone else and keeps you from feeling that eternal connection." Serena paused and looked at him tenderly, understanding how lonely the middling wave must feel. "I know that when you're in a trough and feeling small, every other wave looks like it is high above you and separate from you. But they're not, Dylan; they're as much a part of you as you are of them. The other waves go through troughs just like you do, and most of them feel just as sad and alone as you do. That's another connection that you share."

Dylan pondered the idea for several minutes, his brow furrowed in concentration. He frowned as he recalled the impending shore. The roar of the other waves crashing onto the sand reverberated more loudly by the minute. When he finally spoke, it was with a tone of frustration.

"I'm not sure what the point is of learning this now. I'm going to crash in a short time and it will all be over."

"It's never over, Dylan," Serena said. "That's what I've been trying to tell you."

"You mean we're not going to crash?" he asked, hoping she was correct.

"Of course we're going to crash. All waves crash. It's the way things are," she said. "But crashing is not the end. It is a new beginning!"

"I don't understand," Dylan said. "Whether we're one or not, I am going to smash onto the shore soon. I will scatter into a million droplets that will never come back together the same way. There won't be enough left of me to douse a hermit crab, let alone begin again!"

"Oh, Dylan. You still don't get it, do you. You are not a mere wave who will be lost forever when you crash on the shore. *You are the ocean, perfect and eternal.*" Serena smiled gloriously.

"The whole thing?" he asked, still struggling to comprehend the idea, hopeful and a bit fearful at the thought.

"Every droplet, every wave, every peak, and every trough is reflected in you. You are the ocean and the ocean is you. This middling wave you think you are is just a temporary container, Dylan. Thinking you're just a wave is like the sky thinking it is only a gust of wind. That's why I tell you that crashing on the shore is so wonderful—you get to reconnect with who you truly are!"

Dylan felt thrilled and overwhelmed at the same time. "It can't...it just can't be!" he sputtered.

"And yet it is," Serena said.

In the distance, Dylan heard the plaintive echo of a pod of pilot whales; their beautiful song reverberated through him and seemed to resonate with Serena's words. Then Dylan felt the most incredible feeling as a deep, ancient knowing swept through him, and he knew that what Serena said was *true*. Dylan began to tremble with awe and wonder.

Suddenly, one of the whales near Dylan and Serena broke the surface in a slow, graceful arc, like the rising of a huge gray moon. The whale looked at Dylan for several moments without blinking, and then turned slowly to Serena.

"Serena! My favorite wave in the whole ocean!" The whale smiled with obvious pleasure. Serena smiled happily in return and swept across the mammal's huge glistening back in a gentle embrace.

"Walter, I'd like you to meet my new friend, Dylan." She turned toward the middling wave. "Dylan, this is Walter, one of my dearest old friends."

"Hi, um, hello. How do you do?" Dylan nervously touched the pilot whale's back in a tentative greeting. The whale's massive body dwarfed him as he rolled languorously between Dylan and Serena.

"Glad to meet you, Dylan," Walter said. Then he turned back to Serena. "My pod felt a strong reverberation under the water just now. Any idea what that was all about?"

"As a matter of fact, I do," Serena smiled mysteriously. She nodded toward Dylan with a look of pride on her crest and said, "My new friend here just realized his connection to the ocean!"

"Well, happy birthday!" Walter roared; his thunderous voice caused Dylan to bob violently up and down.

Dylan looked puzzled. "But it's not my birthday," he objected.

"Sure it is!" Walter said. "Today is the day you were born into the real world. It's like a second chance at life—a new beginning!" His broad, smooth gray forehead suddenly creased in a frown. "If I'd known it was your birthday I would have gotten you a present...." He thought for a moment. "I know! I'll give you a baby shower!" Walter dived back beneath the waves and quickly resurfaced. Without warning, he blew as hard as he could from his blowhole, showering Dylan in a cascade of rainbow-colored droplets.

Dylan laughed with delight as the spectrum of colors glistened around him. He danced joyfully in their midst, captivated by the way the droplets in his wave reflected the greens and blues and violets of the rainbows.

When the mist settled, Dylan grinned at Walter and Serena. "That was the coolest birthday present I ever received. Thank you so much!"

Walter winked one gigantic eye and smiled. "Congrats, buddy." He looked at Serena. "I've got to get back to my pod, darlin'." He stroked her gently with a massive shiny fin. "I'll catch you soon." Then he turned toward Dylan. "You listen carefully to this wave, now, ya hear?

She taught me everything I know that's worth knowing, and if you're smart, you'll pay close attention."

Dylan nodded his crest vigorously. He wasn't about to disappoint the giant beast. Walter smiled broadly, satisfied with Dylan's response. With a long wink, the pilot whale sank slowly beneath the surface. A few seconds later, Walter reappeared in the distance. Dylan and Serena laughed in delighted response at the shimmering mist skyrocketing into the air as Walter blew his spout once more.

Thoughts to Play With

Life is a series of overwhelming challenges and "ah ha!" moments.

Try to recall a time when a troubling situation led you to discover an important truth or resolution that transformed your life.

Remember how wonderful and empowering the "ah ha" moment felt! Remember how the answers changed the way you saw the world and alerted you to notice the possibilities around you.

Have you ever run into a friend, heard a song, or read something unexpected, which provided the perfect solution to a question or problem with which you were struggling?

Have you ever considered the possibility that this experience was a gift to you from the One?

*D*ylan and Serena watched the majestic mammal disappear on the horizon. Serena turned toward Dylan and had to smile at his awestruck expression. "So birthday boy, what do you think?" she asked playfully.

Birthday boy. Dylan chuckled. "I believe you now, Serena." Then, like the sun passing behind a cloud, his expression darkened. "But just knowing that I'm one with everything doesn't make me feel less afraid about crashing on the shore."

"It doesn't have to be a scary experience, Dylan. You can choose to see the shore in a different way; you can even be happy about what awaits you," Serena explained in a reasonable tone.

"Happy. Are you kidding me?" *She's as crazy as a cuttlefish!* he thought. *Poor diluted thing.*

"No, I'm not kidding. You can decide to be happy, just like you have decided to be unhappy right at this moment." Serena saw the shocked look on Dylan's face. "Think about it," she said. "A moment ago you were laughing and happy. Now, just a few seconds later, you feel distressed again."

"I didn't *decide* to be unhappy!" he snapped, bristling at her comment. "I don't have any choice! I'm about to be crushed and that's not a reason to celebrate."

"Well, I'm about to crash too, but I'm very happy because I choose to be," she countered. "The choice is entirely mine, just as it is yours."

"That's easy for you maybe, but you're obviously wiser than I am or you wouldn't be so big and beautiful. I don't have the same knowledge and insight, so I don't have the same ability to choose that you do," Dylan argued defensively.

"Things are only 'good' or 'bad' because we label them that way, Dylan," Serena chided him. "It's all about how we choose to perceive things, and I choose to see the shore as another exciting adventure. You see, my friend, everything we think about and everything we do is because we see the world in a certain way—the way we want things to be." She leaned toward Dylan and smoothed the frown from his crest in a loving gesture. Serena then continued, "Sometimes the things that happen may look bad at first glance, but really, our experiences offer us the opportunity to push ourselves to greater peaks." Serena leaned protectively around Dylan and tried to reason with him. "An easy life may seem nice, but choppy waters prepare us for the inevitable storms that *will* come our way, regardless of whether we are small, or middling, or great."

"I still don't see why I should be happy about it," Dylan pouted.

"If you choose to focus on the negative, you will look for things that reinforce that negative view." Serena drew Dylan's attention to a small group of sharks prowling for dinner. "Do you see those sharks?"

Dylan shivered apprehensively. He and Serena watched as a tiger shark savagely attacked an unsuspecting tuna. The shocking encounter sickened and disturbed the middling wave.

Serena let out a sad sigh. "The main thing those sharks care about is finding and devouring food—almost any sea creature will do," she noted. "They are so focused on this one task that all they see around them are potential prey. The sharks don't notice the beauty of the sunrise or the gentle tug of the tides. When they see a dolphin, these predators don't admire its nimble antics or appreciate its playful nature; they only see an easy meal."

Serena paused, noting Dylan's perplexed expression. "What I'm trying to say, Dylan, is that what we focus on becomes our reality. If I choose to focus on the excitement of my life journey, as I do, I see wonderful possibilities all around me," she explained. "But if all I thought about were scary hurricanes or mean sharks or the impending

shore, I would spend all my time being afraid and never

see any of the wonders around me." Serena raised her

foamy brow. "I choose happiness. What do you choose,

Dylan?"

Dylan's crest drooped with exasperation. "It's just

not that easy, Serena," he protested. "I don't have any

control over what happens to me, and I can't just *choose*

happiness when something bad happens!"

"But you *can*, Dylan, and you must understand that

you *do* have a choice if you want to have real happiness

in your life." Serena could see by his doubtful expression

that he didn't believe her. "Let's take an example from

your everyday experience," she suggested. "How would you feel if another wave intentionally came crashing down on you?"

"I'd be mad and upset, of course!"

"All right. Now what if, after the other wave crashed into you, you realized he had actually been blocking you from an even bigger, more destructive wave?"

The middling wave shrugged. "Well, then I'd be happy and grateful."

"So, the same wave crushes you in exactly the same manner and you are just as shaken up, but you have two different responses—all depending on how you *perceive* what happened and how you *label that experience*," she declared.

"Okay, I can see your point there, but I still don't see how I can feel anything but anger if I think the other wave was trying to hurt me," he persisted.

"Do you want to feel angry and upset, or do you want to be happy and content?" Serena asked him.

Dylan looked at her as if she was crazy. "I want to be happy and content, obviously!"

"Do you want other waves to decide whether you're happy or not?" Serena pressed him.

"Of course not!" Dylan shook his crest adamantly, flinging foamy gray specks in all directions.

"Then don't give them that power!" Serena said emphatically. "No matter what life or other waves do to you, they can't force you to be unhappy. They can't force you to feel *anything*! You are the only one who controls what happens inside your mind. If you want to feel happy and content, you have to exert your free will and reshape the way you label the things that happen to you."

Without notice, a distressed gannet plopped down into Dylan's wave and let out a loud burp, regurgitating a nasty blob of plastic from a discarded soda bottle.

"Euww!" Dylan exclaimed, splashing at the bird to make him leave.

"'Scuse me," the goose-like gannet murmured in embarrassment, immediately taking back to the air and leaving Dylan floating with the slobbery mess.

"Ptooey! That was disgusting!" He rolled from side to side like a deranged eel, trying to dislodge the plastic from his wave.

Serena suppressed a smile. "Quick, Dylan," she challenged, "how do you choose to feel, right now, right at this moment?"

"I feel yucky and polluted!" he complained crabbily. "And I feel ticked off at that stupid bird for using me as his personal trash barge."

"*OR,*" Serena said, "you can think back to a time when you got seasick too, and then choose to feel sorry for the poor thing because he was choking on someone else's pollution." She gave him a wise look and said, "You could even be grateful that the gannet came along just in time to teach you a lesson you're trying to learn."

Dylan was aghast. *Grateful? For what?* He grew quiet for a minute, bobbing thoughtfully beside his friend, thinking about how unhappy and distressed the gannet looked. When he thought about it, he really did feel sorry for the little guy; it wasn't fun being sick. He thought harder, trying to see the lesson Serena was trying to awaken within him. Dylan looked skyward and sighed with exasperation. "Okay. I give up. What's the lesson?"

"The lesson, my friend, is that anything can happen at any time, but if you choose to look for the positive, or at the very least, a rational explanation for the things that happen to you, you won't get yourself into a squall over every little thing and you'll be a lot happier." Serena flung her foam into the air as if to say, "Ta da!"

Dylan had to smile. Wise and gracious, Serena really was a wonderful teacher, and he felt lucky to be counted as her friend. "Still," Dylan said fretfully, "there are some feelings I can't avoid, like being afraid of hurricanes. They're so big and scary and destructive!"

"I know." Serena nodded in agreement, recalling her own fears as a younger wave. "They really are. But Dylan, life is full of scary things. No wave is free of them. I was terrified of them myself when I was a wavelet."

"But not now?" he asked, a tone of awe in his voice.

"Nope, not anymore. You see, one night, right smack in the middle of a terrible storm, I was screaming my fool crest off in fear when an old friend of mine, a sea turtle named Eve, popped her wrinkly head above my wave to see what all the fuss was about. I told her I was afraid, and do you know what she told me?"

Dylan shook his crest. He listened intently, hanging on her every word.

"Eve looked at me with surprise and asked why I was so upset. 'The storm will end soon and you'll be okay,' she said. 'You just have to ride it out.'   I argued with her and said, 'But I don't know that for sure! I could be totally flattened by the next big wind gust!' I was so petrified I could hardly hear her over the screams in my head. 'Well, then, why be upset?' Eve asked again. 'You can't do anything about the storm; it will happen whether you worry or not. So spare yourself that extra bit of agony and focus your energy on dealing with whatever happens next. Besides,' Eve added, 'you never know when the wind will blow your way and turn the whole thing around.'"

"That's awesome, Serena!" Dylan was amazed at the perfect timing of Eve's appearance. "Eve showed up right when you needed her!"

"And Eve was right!" Serena concluded. "I haven't bothered with worry since. I can't tell you how much happier I am now that I don't drown myself in worry and self-pity."

"Wow. What a cool story," Dylan raved. "I wish I could do that!"

"You can!" Serena encouraged him. "That's what I'm trying to tell you. If you learn to reshape the way you think about things, you can eliminate most of your suffering."

Thoughts to Play With

What we focus on becomes our reality. We alone decide whether to be happy; no one can *force* us to feel anything.

Even in the most difficult situations, we always have a choice about how we respond, spiritually, mentally, emotionally and physically.

Think of a challenge you are facing right now that worries you.

You can change your perspective by giving different words and descriptions to your situation. For example, instead of seeing a choice you must make as overwhelming or scary, try to see it as an opportunity to make a positive change for yourself and others.

With a fresh perspective, you can focus your energy on handling the situation as it unfolds, rather than feeling worried or afraid.

Notice the support that flows into your life when your positive thoughts attract solutions and opportunities.

$\mathcal{D}$ylan felt a school of brilliant orange and white clownfish wriggle through him on their way to a nearby reef. He laughed as they tickled him, and they wriggled even harder at the happy sound. Dylan loved to cavort with his little ocean friends, and he let out a friendly roar to make his wave vibrate and tickle the clownfish in return. After his amusing little friends swam away, Dylan said earnestly, "I really do want to be happy. I'm just not sure what that means. After all, I feel happy when I reach a nice peak, but then the happiness disappears with the next trough."

"That's because you're confusing happiness with mere pleasure," Serena said.

"What's the difference?" Dylan was genuinely perplexed.

"There's a big difference between the two," Serena declared. She paused, rolling quietly next to the middling wave as she decided how to explain. Then she continued, "Pleasure is a fleeting feeling of satisfaction that comes with getting something you want, like a wave peak, or avoiding something you don't want, like a trough. But happiness—genuine, lasting happiness—isn't a sensation; it's a state of mind." Serena floated closer to Dylan. "It's knowing that every experience holds a gift for you in its hands, if only you will open your heart and mind to receive it."

"But you're so much bigger than I am! You aren't constantly being tossed around like I am. You have fewer things to worry about, so it's easier for you to be happy," he countered.

"Dylan, *every wave* is fighting a heroic battle, the same as you are. Every wave goes through storms and troughs. All waves have their peaks and valleys, and their lows are just as depressing as yours are, and their peaks are just as exhilarating. Even if they're not the same height or depth as yours, they're just as powerful." Serena's voice was reasonable and convincing. Dylan realized she was right.

"You can't judge a wave by the size and beauty of its crest," she continued. "As I shared earlier, the experiences you and I have may be different, and we may appear different on the surface, but otherwise we are exactly the same."

Dylan heaved a great sigh. It was all so complicated. So very *different* from everything he had ever been taught.

"The truth is, *no* wave really controls anything outside his own mind," Serena explained. "We do things that affect others, but even when we think the results are obvious, life has a funny way of following its own plan. Like my sea turtle friend Eve said, life gets so much lighter, so much easier, when you give up worrying about everything. Besides," the beautiful wave added, "most of our emotions are just a tempest in a tide pool."

Dylan's foam shook with a rueful laugh. "Okay, I do let myself get in a swell about things."

"My friend, you and every other wave let yourselves get into a swell because you're so attached to having things go your way. You want to achieve great peaks, but storms thwart you, so you get upset. You want to avoid the troughs, but other waves push you down, so you get upset." Serena checked the smaller wave's expression to see if he was following her. "Things are only perfect a fraction of the time, Dylan. This means that most of your life is spent being miserable about what you don't have and frantically seeking what you want to have. It's a terrible and sad way to live."

Serena paused to allow a pelican to scoop a fish from her generous belly. She lowered her wave as much as she could to make it easier for him, leaving Dylan a bit higher than she was for a moment. In that instant, Dylan realized that other waves, even big beautiful ones, had their low points too. But it was obvious that even though Serena was in a trough, she was very content. His eyes grew large with amazement and he drew in a sharp breath. Maybe she was right; maybe it was possible to *choose* to be happy.

"Oh, Serena!" Dylan whispered, delighted and regretful at the same time, his intense green eyes on the beautiful wave. "Why didn't I know this sooner?"

When the pelican had retrieved its trophy, Serena said, "You didn't see it before because you have lived your life on the surface, focused on superficial things—how choppy the water is; how black the clouds are. Your awareness and understanding only skim the surface, and you can't see how things really are—meaning, you don't appreciate that you are the ocean." She watched Dylan closely to make certain he was following her. "This constant cycle of clinging and running away blocks your happiness and progress," Serena continued. "It makes you selfish, because you want things *your* way. You're so focused on making this happen, that if other waves get in your way; you just push them aside or run them over. You become like a riptide that drowns everything in its path."

Dylan blushed with shame and curled up on himself. He realized she was right; he did spend most of his time trying to get his way, even to the point of manipulating other waves to get what he wanted.

"Why do I do that?" he asked sheepishly.

"Don't feel badly; most waves do the exact same thing," Serena assured him. "Selfish waves are starving waves. They crave superficial things because they believe it will make them happy, finally, for good. These waves either don't know any better or they don't believe there's anything better to reach for," she said. "Starving waves wrongly believe that selfishness is the only way to get what they need. The problem is they're looking 'out there' for what they want, when happiness can only be generated from within." Serena shook her crest sadly. "This kind of negative, selfish thinking and acting choke the ocean more than environmental pollution ever could."

Dylan was startled at the idea that negative thoughts could harm the ocean more than the disgusting trash he had seen along his journey. He knew that environmental pollution was killing his beloved ocean and his friends as well. Immediately he thought about a massive oil spill that he'd once seen that littered the sea with the dying bodies of fish and waterfowl. In his mind, he heard the heart-wrenching cries of the creatures and the waves as they struggled to escape the black, tarry petroleum. His anguish was so great that he felt as if it was happening to him too. With an aching heart, Dylan recalled how he was powerless to save his friends. Barely able to hold back the tears, Dylan shared his sad memory with Serena.

"Oh, Dylan, I'm so sorry," Serena empathized. Her wise eyes were filled with pain and compassion for Dylan and for the poor creatures that spent their last moments trapped in the oil slick. "How terribly sad that you had to see your friends suffer so."

The memory had shaken Dylan to the core and he felt a fresh wave of anger. "How can you say that selfishness is the biggest problem? I can't see how it hurts anyone but ourselves, whereas pollution can kill us all!"

"Yes," Serena agreed. "Trash can choke the ocean, but selfishness, negativity, anger, and hatred, damage the very *soul of the ocean*, of our collective being. And *your* anger and hatred and selfishness are part of the problem," she stressed. "Until you recognize this and decide to change it, the ocean will get more and more soul sick, until it is destroyed," Serena said emphatically.

Dylan reared up his wave and bobbed stiffly on the water. "I'm hardly ever angry!" he protested hotly. "How can my little bit of anger, which is justifiable, by the way, ruin the whole ocean? I know other waves who are mean and hurtful, but I'm not like that!" Dylan insisted. His angry breathing churned his wave until it was almost nothing but froth.

Serena shook her head sadly. "Cruelty, hatred, and anger are always hurtful. Always. Even if you don't project them onto other waves, at the very least they diminish you. Hatred and anger are the most destructive emotions of all," Serena explained, looking intently at Dylan. "They are almost always based on ignorance or fear, and they *always* contribute to the ocean of suffering."

Serena's words took the wind out of Dylan's sails and his crest drooped. "What do you mean 'they *always* contribute to the ocean of suffering'? What's that?" he asked.

Serena began patiently, "Imagine that the life force of the universe is an abundant ocean of life flowing through time. All beings are part of this ocean. In its natural form, the water is pristine and clear. But just as some creatures have physically polluted the oceans on the planet, each of us has added to the pollution of the ocean of life with our negative emotions and actions." Serena watched Dylan carefully, knowing this was the most difficult concept for any wave to grasp.

Dylan was quiet for several long seconds. He knew Serena was wise and he certainly trusted her, but it was uncomfortable and even painful to consider that his actions actually made the situation worse. He watched absentmindedly as a fluther of jellyfish wafted past. Dylan let out a sigh of confusion and trepidation.

Looking at him with compassion, Serena continued in a gentle voice, "Every other wave and sea creature is a mirror of you, Dylan. What you see around you is who you are. We can't blame other waves for causing the pollution because *we* are part of the problem."

Dylan narrowed his eyes and looked rebellious for a moment, wanting to reject Serena's logic.

The big wave looked sternly at Dylan from above. "It's a lot more comfortable and convenient to believe the responsibility lies with other waves, but if you honestly examine your thinking and pay attention to the thoughts and the words that flow from you, you'll realize that you are just as responsible as they are."

Dylan frowned and looked troubled. "I don't like the idea that I'm part of the problem."

"The ocean of life didn't get polluted by itself, my friend. It got that way because each of us contributes our own polluted thoughts and actions. Over time, the ocean of life has become black with hatred, greed, and jealousy. This terrible form of pollution chokes every living thing, and in the same way we view the environmental pollution around us, we tend to believe that others are the problem, not us," Serena said with regret in her voice.

"But how can I not react to other waves and sea creatures when they try to harm me or others I care about?" Dylan pleaded, genuinely wanting to learn this most important of lessons.

"Look within, Dylan. If you are polluted by negativity, you will attract negativity to you—it's the law of the ocean," Serena said. "Your actions affect every wave around you. Negativity is like the wind; it moves you whether it is a hurricane or a tiny gust. The problem is, we can't see our mental pollution, so we don't recognize the damage it does to us all," she offered in a reasonable tone.

Serena tossed a strand of foam from her eyes and tried another tack. "Dylan, have you ever noticed that when you're in a trough, feeling crabby, that other waves don't seem quite as nice to you?"

Dylan nodded. Just yesterday, he had been in the doldrums, and it seemed like every other wave was determined to keep him down.

Serena continued, "And have you noticed that when you're at a peak, you don't like having your happiness spoiled by some grumpy little creature, and that when you bump up against an angry or anxious wave, you begin to lose your joy?"

Dylan nodded again. He certainly didn't appreciate being dragged down by some grouchy, complaining spoilsport. There was nothing like a squawking flock of seagulls fighting over food and dropping frayed feathers into his wave first thing in the morning to ruin his day.

"Negativity is like poison that spreads the more it is shared. Do you see?" Serena momentarily mingled her wave with Dylan's, leaving in her wake a trail of deep blue droplets that colored her beautiful wave.

Dylan looked in wonder as Serena's droplets swirled within his dull green-gray wave. He marveled at how easily both his and Serena's droplets melded into one another, and he realized how negative energy could work the same way.

Thoughts to Play With

Selfishness and negative thinking are at the root of the world's troubles, from poverty to war and terrorism.

Close your eyes and recall your day. Did you shake your fist at a bad driver on the way to work? Did you gossip about someone? Did you feel angry with someone who thwarted you?

Although it is convenient and more comfortable to blame other people, we each contribute to the ocean of suffering through our negative words and actions.

Begin to notice when destructive thoughts run through your mind and try to catch them before they become destructive actions. It takes time and effort, but by doing so, you will be making the world a better place and be closer to manifesting what you desire in your life.

Consider the notion: as we hurt others, we hurt ourselves.

As we uplift others, we uplift ourselves.

*H*appy that he made the connection between the problems in the ocean and his own negativity, Dylan asked, "How can I help make the ocean of life better for all the waves and creatures? How do I stop adding to the pollution?"

The look in Dylan's shining eyes was so earnest, Serena had to smile. "To repair the ocean of life, you must understand that *every* negative act is another drop into the polluted water. Every ill thought creates a ripple on its surface that touches the lives of other beings," Serena said. "You must stop adding your own negativity, and do your best to contribute only loving, positive energy to the world."

"Can it really be that easy?" Dylan asked, frowning uncertainly.

"Yes, it can. The most important thing is this: before you take any action or express any thought, ask yourself, 'Am I acting out of love and compassion?' If the answer is yes, then act. If not, refrain." Serena gave a soft smile. "If you do this one simple thing, you will do much to improve the climate of the ocean of life."

Dylan felt a thrill of excitement run through his wave. Then a thought occurred to him. "But I'm just one wave. I can't clean up the ocean by myself!"

"You don't have to do it all by yourself, Dylan." Serena smiled and her eyes sparkled as bright as a sunbeam. "I'm right here with you all the way. There are other creatures out there too who are doing everything they can to make a difference."

"But is it enough?" Dylan asked with concern. "Things seem so bad in the ocean now; what if the negativity wins?" His eyes widened with alarm at the thought.

Serena nodded sagely. "I predict that one day soon, enough waves will realize that their negativity is the number one cause of all the suffering in the world. Then, over time, every wave will become as concerned with their thoughts as they are about the environment."

A clutch of starfish popped up within their waves, like shooting stars, rising up rather than falling from the sky. The starfish peeked between the waves' foam and blinked in the bright sunlight, appearing dazed. Dylan thought they were a good omen and waved goodbye as they descended back to the safety of the cool, dark ocean floor.

Watching Dylan's obvious delight and kindness, Serena smiled to herself. *He is such a wonderful wave.*

Dylan caught her eye and grinned back. "So many sea creatures and waves are so innocent and helpless," he said. "I want to keep them safe. If I ask myself that question, 'Am I acting out of love and compassion,' every time I do something, I'm making the ocean better for them, right?"

"The more you express and share happiness, the better you will feel and make others feel. Happiness creates a cycle that feeds on itself, just as negativity does. Whether you choose to live in a positive cycle or a negative one is entirely up to you," Serena stressed. "You can be a negative influence and increase the pollution, or you can be a positive influence and make the ocean a better place." Serena raised her foamy crest, anticipating his response.

"Well, I certainly don't want to be a negative influence," Dylan responded hastily. He was pensive for a moment, watching the sea birds circle and dive in the water. Finally, he returned his attention to his mentor. "Serena, I still don't understand how I can think positively about the things that make me angry or afraid." He fumbled for the right words to explain how strongly he felt. "When I'm struggling to stay together in the middle of a storm or I'm so low I can't see the horizon, all I feel is fear and despair." He peered anxiously at the sky for any sign of thunderclouds. He spotted a tiny cloud and felt a flurry of anxiety, wondering if it would grow into a real threat.

"We are one even with the storms, Dylan. In fact, troughs and storms make us stronger and prepare us for even greater challenges. They push us toward places in our mind and spirit where we would never go voluntarily," she said. "Nature's troughs and storms will end, and then they will come again. If you see them as part of the cycle of life, as part of yourself, you can appreciate how your own stormy thoughts rise and fall. You can become more tolerant and patient with them. You can ride them out calmly, knowing they'll blow over soon."

Dylan carefully considered her words. It was hard to accept that he was one with the troughs and storms, and even more difficult to imagine riding out their tumultuous drama with calm.

Serena understood his expression and asked, "Have you ever experienced a storm that didn't end?"

Dylan shook his crest.

"Of course not, and you never will," she said. "You must remember that the sun is always shining above the fiercest hurricane."

Serena's voice was soothing and reassuring, and Dylan found himself beginning to believe that troughs and storms might not be the end of the world after all. "I know that's true, but in the middle of a storm I forget," he said.

"I understand," she said. "In the midst of our greatest challenges, we forget that we're one with the storm; we see it as our enemy, something to resist, to fight against, rather than something to work through. We have to consciously remind ourselves that we are a part of it, and don't have to struggle against it all alone."

"But if I don't fight it, I could be destroyed!" Dylan exclaimed. Foam flew from his crest.

"True, you must do your best to survive, but realize that most of your efforts are futile. Your energy would be better spent collaborating with other waves to stay safe, rather than fighting just for your own survival. If you all help one another, then every wave gets what it needs to survive and be happy.

"But," the elegant wave warned, "as long as you think only of yourself and ignore the needs of others, you'll never be satisfied, because you'll be competing with all the other waves for the same resources. In fact, to be really happy, you must make the needs of others your greatest focus."

Thought to Play With

Many people work to make the world a better place, and you can too.

Ask yourself, "Am I acting out of love?" before you take action, and you can be certain your efforts will lead to positive results.

The more you express and share happiness, the better you will make others feel; and the cycle goes on and on from one person to the next.

Think of someone you helped recently and recall how wonderful it made you feel to know you were improving their life and increasing their happiness.

Make a commitment to help three people every day and happiness will fill your life.

*D*ylan liked the idea of helping others, but a disturbing thought occurred to him. "But surely if I give all my attention and energy to other waves I will be left with nothing!"

"On the contrary," Serena said, bringing Dylan closer to her to comfort him. "You will find you have more happiness and attention than you could ever want. Cherishing others is the greatest thing you can do to end your own suffering. When you put other waves first, you'll find that you always get your needs met in the process. In fact, the more you give to others the more you will receive in return."

Dylan tilted his crest and looked surprised. "But how could that be?"

"Think about it. Let's say you are surrounded by a handful of other waves of varying size. There's a terrible hurricane coming. The winds are whipping the waves around so violently that they threaten to destroy you all. Your only hope is to be bigger and more powerful than the wind. If you tried to take care of just yourself, you would certainly perish. But if every wave combined into one super wave, all of you could ride out the storm safely,"

Serena said. "Not only would you be safer, you would feel less afraid with so many other waves supporting you. That makes sense, doesn't it?" She watched his expression.

Dylan nodded thoughtfully. It did make sense. During the monster hurricane last year, he had survived only because he had hidden within a larger group of waves. He told Serena about his experience and admitted how relieved he was not to be alone during the storm.

Recalling her own experiences as a younger wave, Serena smiled knowingly. "When you meet the needs of others, you will get your own needs met and find real happiness. Help other waves reach their own peaks, and in the process, you will reach your peak too. That's the real secret of our purpose in this ocean, Dylan—to help others, and cherish them as much as we do ourselves," she smiled kindly. "You see, in the act of giving, you become your highest self, Neptune-like, and you actualize your true nature."

Dylan suddenly spotted an exhausted red-eyed vireo that dropped like a rock into the water nearby. The tiny songbird had been blown out to sea and gotten lost. The poor creature was totally spent and discouraged, and its trembling olive wings could fly no farther. Dylan's heart ached for the little fellow, and he knew that without something to perch on to keep the bird afloat, he would drown. Dylan spotted a flat piece of driftwood close by, and thinking quickly, scooped the vireo onto the board. Then he rolled with all his might to propel the driftwood toward a nearby island where the bird could rest until he was able to fly back home. Dylan was enormously happy that he could help someone, and he felt happy with himself for finding such a quick solution.

Serena smiled proudly as she watched Dylan help the struggling bird. Then she looked toward the shore and wondered if they had time to complete their conversation before they crashed. She wanted very much for Dylan to reach his full potential during his journey, and she sent a silent prayer for his success.

Dylan interrupted her musings when another thought occurred to him. "Serena, if helping others to be happy makes me happy, how is that not being selfish?" he asked.

"There's nothing wrong with wanting to be happy. That's a good thing," she assured him. "Even if that's the only reason you help others at first, that's a good start. Over time, as you see how your actions help others, your happiness will not only grow, but your desire to help them will become stronger than the desire to please yourself. By valuing yourself, you value everything around you, and by valuing the creatures around you, you come to value yourself. It's a wonderful symbiotic relationship."

Dylan realized that he did feel happier and better about himself after he helped someone else. "So what's the best way to help others?" he asked.

"One of the most powerful ways is to appreciate them," Serena offered. "Every wave longs to be appreciated; this deep longing drives most of our actions. If you show and tell others that you value and respect them, the response will be overwhelming. They'll appreciate and respect you in return for making them feel valued and for encouraging their efforts to be happy themselves."

Dylan frowned. "But not every wave deserves appreciation or respect," he objected, thinking of a number of waves who had tried to crush him.

"Nevertheless, you must remember that no matter how self-defeating others' behavior appears, they're also trying to find happiness and love, just like you are," Serena said. "When that's not available to them, they lash out instead, hurting themselves and others in the process. Even waves who behave badly crave appreciation and respect as much as anyone, but they're hindered by their negative view of the world."

"Why is that?"

"I think it's because these waves believe either that they don't deserve to be happy, and even if they do, they tend to think that happiness is something they have to obtain from the outside," Serena offered. "Every wave is worthy, whether they believe it or not. If you can be appreciative and respectful to each wave no matter whom they are, you'll be amazed by how they respond. Not all of them, but most will be truly grateful, and you will be a better wave for the effort."

Dylan wasn't certain he agreed that every wave was worthy; still, he knew Serena wouldn't steer him wrong. He decided to give his new mentor the benefit of the doubt, and told her he would try to be more patient with the rough waves he encountered.

Serena continued. "You see, Dylan, if you think like the soul of the ocean that you are, you will be able to see everything and every wave as perfect and complete and striving for the same purpose." Serena's eyes sparkled and she said, "I hope you realize by now that you already possess everything you need to be happy—right here, right now, in this very moment."

"So if I really want to be happy, I have to help others." Dylan repeated Serena's words to cement the concept in his mind. He grew pensive. "But whether or not I'm really the ocean, right now I'm just a middling wave rolling haplessly toward the shore. What possible difference can I make?"

"We shape the world through our collective power, but even one tiny wave, given enough time, can carve a canyon in the rocks." Serena offered a tender smile of encouragement. "Your positive attitude will reverberate and encourage others to give their best, too." Serena went on, "When you give to others, you'll find you don't need the peak experiences to be happy because you will be constantly creating happiness for yourself. And, when you give to others, the love just grows bigger and stronger, on and on." Serena stroked Dylan's crest fondly. "It is your true purpose for being."

Dylan watched her with eyes wide with wonder. "It is?"

"Yes, and it's the same purpose for all of Neptune's creatures. The goal is to achieve your fullest potential and recognize your true nature—that is to say, that you truly are the ocean. Once you realize this, you will never again think of yourself as a mere wave, but as the powerful and eternal ocean you really are."

Thoughts to Play With

Magically, when we meet the needs of others, we get our own needs met in the process. The best way to help others is to *appreciate them.*

How do you feel when no one appreciates you for your efforts?

How wonderful do you feel when people *do* tell you they appreciate you?

Today, express appreciation for three other people—at home or at work—and you will find that they will appreciate you in return.

Our highest purpose is to achieve our fullest potential and recognize our true nature. Help others to find their true nature and you will find your own.

"*I* want so much to believe you, but I don't know how," Dylan cried plaintively. His eyes pleaded with Serena to help him make the connection that he knew was there, but couldn't seem to grasp.

Serena rolled up close beside him and wrapped her wave around him in a gentle, loving embrace. "It's very simple. Just stop wallowing in your own drama and look around you. See that every wave is seeking happiness, just as you are. Do whatever you can to help other waves find happiness and you'll find yourself being happy too. You'll begin to understand the direct relationship between the happiness of others and your own happiness. Then you'll know all waves are the same." Her smile beamed at him.

Dylan closed his eyes and basked in a feeling of connection with every being in the ocean.

"Tell me, Dylan, if you knew, I mean *really* understood your true nature and that you are *one* with every other being in the ocean, how would you change the way you live?"

Dylan bobbed thoughtfully for several minutes, his crest furrowed in concentration. "Well, I would certainly be happier, and I would worry a lot less." He paused. "I would be kinder to myself and others," he continued. "I would treat every wave as precious and try to help them realize their true nature. And I would stop thinking so much about myself and what I want and more about what is best for all beings."

There was a long pause before Serena asked gently, *"So what's stopping you?"*

With those simple words, Dylan felt a seismic shift within. He suddenly grasped the concepts Serena had been trying to teach him. He saw that he really *did* have the power to reshape his thinking and to see himself and the ocean around him differently. Dylan realized and accepted that the ocean didn't revolve around him and his dramas. And just as he knew the wind and the ocean weren't out to get him, Dylan realized they didn't owe him anything either. He was completely responsible for his own suffering and his own happiness. He saw that by changing his perspective, he could reshape his reality and find true, lasting happiness.

Suddenly Dylan felt ten feet tall! Then the most amazing thing happened. As Dylan's mind expanded with these realizations, his wave grew bigger in response. With wonder and tears of joy in his eyes, Dylan looked at his massive, beautiful, brilliant blue wave, now glowing with enlightenment.

With growing amazement, Dylan shared his realization with Serena, telling her how the wisdom she shared had touched his heart and transformed his thinking.

"That was magnificent!" Serena roared proudly. "*You are magnificent!*" She combined her wave with Dylan's, and the two of them towered over the ocean, taking him higher than he had ever dreamed.

Dylan looked around in amazement. He could see the scarlet sun melting into the horizon. He could see the tops of the other big, beautiful waves around him. He could see the shore up ahead, and for the first time he wasn't terrified of reaching it.

Turning back toward the sinking sun, Dylan watched in awe as the moon rose at the same time. The moon and the sun together against the tangerine sky were achingly beautiful. A lump rose in his throat.

Dylan reveled in the greatest wave peak he had ever achieved, knowing he only made it with the help of his friend. He looked lovingly at Serena and thanked her from the bottom of his heart for making his dream come true.

Serena smiled back. She was grateful to Dylan, too, for allowing her to share her energy and wisdom with him. Nothing made her happier than helping other waves discover their true nature.

Serena continued to lift Dylan until the sun slipped below the horizon, and the moon rose gloriously in the sapphire sky.

Thoughts to Play With

If you truly understood your true nature and that you are one with every other being, how would you change the way you live?

Would you be less selfish?

Would you be kinder to others and to yourself?

Would you spend more time trying to help others?

Would you be happier?

So what's stopping you?

"Dylan," Serena said softly.

Dylan looked at her, his face brilliant with joy.

"It's time," she said simply.

Dylan looked down at the shore, so close now he could see the foam of fallen waves sink into the sandy beach. His heart was so filled with gratitude and wonder that he had no room for fear. He gave thanks for his life, for his family and friends, for high wave peaks, and yes, for hurricanes, for all his teachers—especially Serena—

and for the promise of the larger existence that awaited him on the shore. Whatever this new adventure would bring, Dylan was determined to be a guide for those who were lost at sea, to reunite them with their true nature, as Serena had done for him.

Dylan looked at Serena and met her eyes. They smiled joyfully at each other.

"I love you," he told her. His eyes were radiant with happiness.

Serena drew Dylan close, in a final, loving embrace. "I love you, too."

Just as he and Serena crested for the last time, Dylan saw a flash of electric blue light shoot across the crest of their waves. It was the most enchanting sight he had ever seen. The middling wave had heard that when the moon was just right, the phosphorus in the waves caught the light and sent neon blue shivers rippling across the crests. The incredible shimmering light was like a parting gift from Neptune.

Both Dylan and Serena's bodies crashed onto the shore, churning chaotically, rushing, rushing, rushing forward. Their intermingled droplets fanned out and slipped quietly back into the open and welcoming arms of the ocean.

∾

All traces of Dylan and Serena were gone. Their once powerful waves, now millions of scattered droplets, drifted low across the ocean floor.

The ocean smiled and embraced the enlightened droplets. An undertow ushered them back out to sea, where they would be combined with other droplets to form new waves. Many of the new waves would live their brief lives trapped in the lie of their separateness, but a rare and precious few would spend their time helping other waves discover who they really are.

As a strong breeze ruffled the water's glistening surface, a voice on the wind offered a whispered promise to the ocean, "One day you will learn that you are not merely the ocean—you are also the sun and the moon

and the infinite universe itself."

The ocean smiled again. It could hardly wait.

The End

Acknowledgments

I would like to express my deepest gratitude to the following people:

- To my husband, Wes, the most devoted and supportive man on the planet.

- To my children, Sean, Steven, and Amy, for teaching me about love.

- To my parents, Walter and Ruth Gray, for giving me this precious life, and to my mother for her essential feedback on this book.

- To my in-laws, Howard and Jimmie Lee Walters, for loving me like their own daughter.

- To my twin brother, Walt, for being his wise, wonderful self.

- To my sister, Wendy, for her keen eyes and optimism.

- To my editor, Irene Lucas, whose creativity, skill and enthusiasm polished the dross of this book into gold, and whose delightful sense of fun brought the characters to life.

- To my dearest friends, Barbara Brigham, Tracy Crow, Charlotte Carraher, Debbie Friedman, Lisa Miles Brady, Tinlay and Dekey Palden, and Tenzin Tinley.

- To my supporters from the Kadampa Center, Geshe Gelek Chodak and Julie LaValle Jones.

- To the most knowledgeable and compassionate physician in the world, the man who saved my life, Dr. Charles Beauchamp.

About the Author

CJ Scarlet's life fell apart after learning she had a life-threatening illness. Then a Tibetan lama led her on a journey that tapped her innate wisdom and spirituality to find the secret of true happiness. What she learned transformed her life and miraculously healed her mind, body, and spirit. Today, CJ's illness is in remission, and she has achieved greater happiness than she ever dreamed.

To teach others how simple it is to spread kindness, happiness and gratitude, CJ will launch the **Kindness Cure Campaign** on World Kindness Day, Nov. 13, 2008. Over the next year CJ will:

- **Perform one random act of kindness every day for 365 days**, all of which will be digitally recorded for use online and by the media,
- **Recruit a legion of dedicated volunteers** who perform similar acts in their own communities on the same days,
- **Get 1,000,000 visitors to her Kindness Cure Campaign online community** social media networking site,
- **Share her message of hope** through her speeches, Internet radio program, and media appearances,
- **Help hundreds of people through her coaching program,**
- **Keep a daily blog** on the Kindness Cure website,
- **Stay in touch daily with followers through social networking sites,** like Twitter, Facebook, and MySpace.

CJ Scarlet is an award-winning author, motivational speaker, and certified "Happy Endings" coach, offering happiness tools and inspiration to those who are facing major life challenges.

CJ has 29 years experience in marketing and public relations, and has given speeches and workshops at state, national, and international events. She has appeared on numerous radio and television programs, and was a media spokesperson while serving in the U.S. Marine Corps.

Most recently, CJ was named one of the "Happy 100" people in the U.S., and is featured in the new bestseller, *Happy for No Reason*.

Join CJ's mission to perform one million acts of kindness in one year by becoming a Kindness Bandit and taking action in your own community.
Visit *www.thekindnesscure.org*.

CPSIA information can be obtained
at www.ICGtesting.com
Printed in the USA
FFOW03n0616050118
44359823-44038FF